adventures #2

NICKELODEON
ROCKET POWER

surf's up!

Based on the TV series *Nickelodeon Rocket Power*™
created by Klasky Csupo, Inc. as seen on Nickelodeon®

SIMON SPOTLIGHT

An imprint of Simon & Schuster Children's Publishing Division
1230 Avenue of the Americas, New York, New York 10020

Manufactured in the United States of America

First Edition
2 4 6 8 10 9 7 5 3 1

ISBN 0-689-84556-1

Library of Congress Catalog Card Number: 2001090075

adventures #2

NICKELODEON
ROCKET POWER

surf's up!

by Terry Collins

based on the teleplays by
David Regal and David Rosenberg

3 9082 11185 4876

Simon Spotlight/Nickelodeon

New York   London   Toronto   Sydney   Singapore

story #1
BIG THURSDAY

chapter 1

Most of the time the sun shone brightly on the beaches of Ocean Shores, California, but not today. Today the skies were gray all around, and rain was falling steadily. Even the ocean looked much darker than its usual bluish-green color.

A group of four kids huddled on top of a dune, peering out at the waves smashing against the sand. They were the only ones on the beach.

"There's a storm brewing out there," Reggie

Rocket said. Tall and slender, Reggie was one of those people who took to sports as easily as most people did to eating and breathing.

"Well, duh," her brother, Otto, retorted. "It's gettin' *sooo* gnarly!"

Reggie cocked an eyebrow and folded her arms across her chest. "No way are you serious about trying to go out today, bro. Only a brainless fool would try and ride this surf."

Otto shrugged. "Hey, the Rhino rides these waves. And if the Rhino can, so can I!"

"Excuse me?" Reggie said in disbelief. "The Rhino is only the greatest big-wave surfer there is! And you, well . . . you're . . . you!"

Otto turned from Reggie and slapped Twister on the back. "Hey, Twist! Whaddya say? Let's try it!"

Twister Rodriguez pulled down on his worn cap and shuddered. "I dunno, Otto-man," he said. "Looks kinda wet out there."

Reggie confronted her brother. "See?

Even your best bud thinks it's a bad idea, and he's usually the one who comes up with all the bad ideas."

"Uh . . . yeah," Twister agreed. He was always loyal to Otto, but even he thought surfing in a major storm was not a way to spend an afternoon.

Otto stared at his friend. "Twist! The Twist-a-Thon! Mr. Twister! Stop being so lame! We can do this!"

"Just say no, Twist," Sam Dullard said in a soft voice. Sam was usually quiet and went along with whatever the group decided. But this time even he knew what Otto was proposing was way dangerous.

Otto put an arm around Twister's shoulders and pulled his attention to the crashing waves. "What's wrong with you, man? It's just a little water . . . ," he said temptingly.

"Actually, it's quite a lot of water," Sam

said. "If one does the math—"

Twister interrupted. "Dude, I never was any good at math."

Reggie grabbed Twister and turned him toward her. "Twister," she pleaded. "I want you to think long and hard about this!"

At that instant a massive wave flattened itself on the beach right in front of the gang, covering them with sand and salt water.

"Enough's enough! I'm going inside and getting out of this mess," Reggie said, walking back toward the pier. "Coming?"

Sam fell in step behind Reggie, leaving Otto and Twister still standing on the dune.

"Who needs 'em! You and me, buddy, right?" Otto said.

Twister gulped, then picked up his board and turned to go with Reggie and Sam. "Sorry, Otto," he said, "but I am absolutely *not* going to do this!"

chapter 2

It wasn't long before Otto and Twister were standing at the water's edge.

"So, we're really gonna do this?" Twister asked meekly. He was nervous, but he couldn't let his best friend go out in the water by himself.

"Don't be a wuss," Otto replied. "Just pretend you're taking a bath in a really big tub! You gotta go with the flow!"

Reggie and Sam came back to watch the pair from the sand dune. The storm was now howling along the beach.

"I knew we should have gone inside," Reggie said.

"Ah-choo!" Sam sneezed. "We still can," he said, sniffling.

"Yeah," Reggie said, "but if anything happens to those guys, I want to be there for them."

Otto and Twister were moving along the water's edge with their surfboards. Twister was walking slowly behind Otto, his steps becoming more and more hesitant.

Otto gave his friend a disdainful look. "Twist, these are the kind of waves you dream about," he called. "Now, let's move!"

Otto ran into the violent surf and threw himself onto his surfboard. He began to paddle out toward the crashing waves, glancing back to make sure that Twister was close behind.

Twister sighed and began paddling his

own board across the water. "Oh, man," he muttered worriedly. "This is like, totally bogus!"

"See ya in the lineup!" Otto called as he struggled forward. "Come on, Twist! This is it! Paddle, baby, paddle!"

Twister closed his eyes and paddled frantically, trying to keep pace with Otto. "I promise if I make this wave, I won't talk back to my teachers," he mumbled heaven-ward. "I won't talk back to Lars. I won't talk back to Officer Shirley. I won't even talk back to the movie screen, no matter how bad the flick is!"

Twister opened his eyes in time to see Otto hop to his feet on his surfboard. Behind them the dark green wave began to grow.

From the safety of their dune, Sam and Reggie stared at the size of the wave.

"That's a b-b-big one," Sam stammered.

"Totally," Reggie agreed.

Back on the water Otto stole a glance at Twister. Otto was trying to flash a confident smirk, but Twister could tell that his friend was scared.

Twister, on the other hand, had no heroic illusions. He was terrified.

The two friends stared at each other. What each of them saw in the other's eyes was fear.

"AHHHHHHHHHHHHHHHH!" they screamed in unison.

Reggie and Sam could hear the scream over the sound of the storm.

"I can't look," Sam said, covering his eyes.

"I know," Reggie said, shaking her head sadly. "This is gonna hurt."

Otto and Twister wobbled on their boards at first, but then managed to stand up. They began to ride the wave, even as it grew bigger and bigger.

"Yeah! YEAH!" Otto yelled in triumph. He

was riding the wave! "This is so awesome!"

"I wanna go home!" Twister yelled.

Then, without warning, the wave crashed behind them, kicking up a mountain of grayish-white water that rumbled toward the two surfers. Otto's board lurched to the left, then to the right as the churning waters tried to knock him off his feet.

But Otto stood firm. His feet stuck tight to the board like they were covered in glue, even as the water sent him off course— right into Twister!

CRASH! Both boys flew into the air, their boards vanishing beneath the fast-moving wave. In an instant the water seemed to swallow them up!

"We've got a two-car pileup," Reggie said as Otto and Twister disappeared. "And the wave is still coming in fast!"

"Can you see them?" Sam asked.

Reggie chewed on her bottom lip. "I can't

spot either one of them," she said. "They must still be under. Come on!"

As the torrent of water plunged toward the beach, Reggie and Sam raced toward the wave to try to find their friends. It splashed across the sand, then flowed backward into the ocean.

As the wave retreated all kinds of debris were left behind: driftwood, shells, Otto's cracked surfboard—and the damp forms of Otto and Twister sprawled on the wet sand!

"I'll never be thirsty again," Twister gurgled, spitting out a mouthful of water.

"Are you guys okay?" Reggie asked worriedly.

"I think so," Otto said, coughing.

Reggie checked them over. Amazingly, they were fine. "You guys could have got whomped beyond belief!" scolded Reggie.

"Urrghhh . . . ," Otto moaned.

Twister sat up and held his aching head

in both hands. "You mean we didn't?" he groaned, looking around. "Hey! Where's my board?"

"Long gone," Sam said. "But Otto's came in with the flow!"

"What's left of it, anyway," Reggie added as Otto cradled the damaged board.

"Man, this is so totally bogus," Otto grumbled.

Reggie turned to Twister. "Care to take another crack at those waves?"

"No thanks, man," Twister said. "I'm walking for the rest of the day."

"Good idea," Reggie agreed. "This storm has got to be over by tomorrow."

chapter 3

The next day the gang sat inside the Shore Shack on the pier. Reggie and Otto's father, Ray Rocket, the owner of the restaurant, was with them. So was Tito Makani, Ray's best friend and resident cook.

Ray and Tito had been friends for decades, ever since they started surfing together in the '60s. Ray was an older version of the classic "surfer dude," with broad shoulders and a friendly, laid-back attitude. Tito was born in Hawaii, and was like a father figure to Otto, Reggie, Sam, and Twister.

Obviously, Reggie and Otto got their surfing skills from their father, who was still known to ride a mean board when he put his mind to it.

But there was no surfing today. Everyone was focused on the TV that Tito kept behind the counter. The scene on the screen was the same outside the window—rain, rain, rain—and lots of it!

"That's right," the TV weather reporter announced. "It's the storm of the century! How will we ever survive? Find out tonight . . . at eleven!"

Ray reached over and flicked off the TV. "By tonight, this will all be over . . . I hope," he said, turning to the kids.

"Slow day, huh, Dad?" Reggie said. There were no other customers in the restaurant.

"I guess business is going to be a bit off," Ray agreed, looking at the rampaging storm outside.

"I'll take a pineapple cream soda," Sam said.

Ray gave Sam a cheery wink. "One soda, comin' up!"

While Ray fixed Sam's drink, Tito tried to keep busy. He wiped down the already spotless countertop with a rag. "You know the old Hawaiian saying, 'When surfers don't ride, potatoes aren't fried.'"

Otto gave Tito a cocky smile and put his feet up on a stool. "'When surfers don't ride?' Ha! I've ridden these waves!"

Tito cocked an eyebrow. "*You* were out there, little cuz?"

"Yeah!" Otto said smugly. "What's the big deal?"

"Uh-oh," Twister moaned, wincing at Otto's bragging. "Too much, too soon, dude."

"What's the big deal?!" Ray said, over-hearing the last part of the conversation and plunking down Sam's soda.

Reggie elbowed Otto in the ribs. "Do you like getting in trouble, or do you just have a memory problem?"

Ray placed a firm hand on his son's shoulder. "Listen to me. You're a kid, Otto—and you're not experienced enough. Those waves are out of control!"

Otto gave his father a defiant look. "I can handle it."

Tito shook his head. "That boy. I think he *does* like getting in trouble."

Ray took Otto over to a booth and sat him down for a father-to-son chat. "Otto, you're a good surfer," he said. "But if you want to get better, you have to be smart enough to know your own limitations."

"But, Dad! You don't understand—" Otto protested.

Ray smiled. "Oh, I understand. This reminds me of the time twenty-five years back when Hurricane Monica hit, and I caught the monster killer wave of my life—"

"Cool," Twister said. "I'll bet that was totally insane!"

"—and I wasn't near experienced enough to handle it!" Ray finished, reaching down to rub his left knee in memory of the mighty wave. "Took some major hits that day."

"What happened, Dad?" Reggie asked.

"Did you wipe out?" Sam wondered.

"Ha!" Tito laughed, remembering the day. "You might say that. I saw it myself."

Everyone was now intrigued by Ray's story, and they gathered around the older surfer as he spun his tale.

"When Monica hit, it was right here on this very same beach," Ray said, standing up and acting out the surfer moves as he spoke. "I was on the water, my board under me, and things were looking good. I was higher than I had ever been before on top of that wave, but I couldn't keep my balance. I was tilted forward, and I almost lost it!"

"Almost?" Twister said.

"Almost," Ray replied. "I managed to hold it close, and ended up skidding down the face of that wave at a totally insane speed."

"Way to go, Dad!" Otto cried. "I'll bet you rocked!"

"Sure I did, until that wave got mad and smashed me into the dock!" Ray said, smacking his right fist into the open palm of his left hand. "Not only did I wipe out, but it wiped out the dock as well!"

"Storm waves are unpredictable," Tito said. "Raymundo washed up in a pile of wood and stinky seaweed. Took me half a day to find him."

"Son, I wrote a check my tush couldn't cash," Ray said firmly.

"Yeah! You should have seen his tush bounce," Tito said with a grin. The kids cracked up.

Then Ray got serious again. "And that's why *none of you* are going to surf in this storm!"

Sam took the last swig of his soda and stood up from the counter. "Well, you convinced me," he said nervously. "I'm going home. Gonna sit on the couch, watch some TV, maybe play a video game . . . all nice and dry and safe and sound."

Twister stood up too. "I hear you, dude."

Reggie gave her dad a high five. "You got it, Dad. No surfing!"

Otto wasn't giving up so easily. He pointed to a poster on the front door of the Shore Shack. The poster showed a young barrel-chested dude with long blond hair shooting the curl on a huge wave. "B-But lots of guys surf the big waves!" Otto argued. "What about the Rhino?"

At that instant the door opened, and a barrel-chested dude with long blond hair stepped into the restaurant. "Whoa! Did somebody mention my name?"

chapter 4

Otto gazed in disbelief at the figure that had just entered the Shore Shack. "It-It's the Rhino!" he gasped.

Tito winced and shrugged his shoulders. "Bad timing, bruddah," he whispered to Ray.

Ray rapped the awestruck Otto on the head. "And you're *not* Rhino. Rhino's *a lot* older and *a lot* more experienced."

Otto gazed at his idol. "Dad, he's done it all! Rhino is so totally hardcore."

"Not an exaggeration," the Rhino said with a toothy grin. "I heard the surf's gonna be insane here today. They're calling them the biggest waves of the decade. It's gonna be BIG THURSDAY!"

"You gonna paddle out, Rhino?" Otto asked.

"Hey, that's what I do, little man," Rhino replied.

Ray stepped in front of the Rhino. "Easy on the big stories, Walter. Got it?"

Rhino blushed. "Come on, Ray! Call me Rhino, not Walter! I hate that name!"

Twister snickered. "Walter? Hee-hee-hee!"

Otto frowned and launched his own volley in the war of embarrassing first names. "Hey, watch the name-calling, *Maurice*."

Twister slapped his hands over his ears and winced at the sound of his given name. "Ouch," he said. "Bummer, dude."

The Rhino took a seat at the counter.

"See, to me, big waves are like monsters. Monsters you need to go eye-to-eye with. If you don't face down the monsters, ya might as well boogie board."

"Monsters scare me," Sam said in a small voice.

"They won't if you take them on, man," the Rhino said. "And that's what I'm gonna do right now. Get in a session and pound those waves into submission!"

"The beach is closed, Walter," Ray said.

"Rhino, Ray, call me Rhino!" the surfer replied as he got up to leave. "And hey, they can't padlock a beach! Later, dudes!"

Otto wore a smile that stretched from one side of his head to the other. "How cool is this guy?" he whispered to Twister.

"Cool?" Twister said nervously. He knew from the sound of Otto's voice that their storm-surfing days were far from over.

"Can we go watch him, Dad?" Otto asked.

"No," Ray replied. "If Walter wants to drown himself, that's his business. I don't want any of you to get involved."

"But, Dad!" Otto protested.

"No buts, Otto," Ray replied. He looked at the group of kids. "I want all of you to go home. The beach is not our friend on a day like this. Tito and I will be along in a little while . . . I guess someone had better stay shoreside just in case Walter does get into trouble."

Outside the Shore Shack the storm continued to get worse. A cold wind was blowing, driving the rain down even harder. Otto threw a friendly arm around Twister's shoulders and gave a big fake smile to Reggie and Sam. "I'm going to hang over at the Twist's place. We're going to watch some videos."

"You are?" Twister asked, confused. "We are?"

"You bet! Just like my dad said. We're going indoors and staying away from the beach," Otto said smoothly. He gave his sister a wave. "Later, Reg!"

Reggie and Sam watched the two boys walk away in the storm. "How long you think before they sneak back?" Sam asked.

"As long as it takes them to grab their spare surfboards," Reggie answered. "Come on, we'll hide out and wait for them at the dune we were at yesterday."

Sure enough, in less than ten minutes, Otto and Twister were running back onto the beach, their surfboards held high in an attempt to keep the rain off their heads.

"Do you see him?" Otto asked, searching the beach for the Rhino.

"Man, I can't see much of anything in this rain," Twister replied.

"There he is!" Otto said, pointing out the Rhino across the gloom. "Come on!"

"Dudes!" the Rhino said, giving them a hearty thumbs-up. "I am most glad you could make it!"

"Wouldn't miss seeing you surf for anything!" Otto said. "It's most . . . inspirational."

Twister stayed quiet. He was having trouble standing up in the fierce wind. The rain was drenching him from all directions. He couldn't believe Otto had convinced him into seriously thinking about going out on the water in this mess!

"Ready to witness some real radical surfing?" the Rhino asked as he struck a surfer pose.

"I was going to ask you the same question," Otto said, striking his own version of the same pose.

The Rhino laughed. "Awesome! Enjoy the show!" he said, then turned and ran out into the thrashing waters of the storm-stricken ocean. Otto took a deep breath, ran a hand across his fogged-up eyeglasses, picked up his board, and began to follow. He had just stepped into the water when a voice cried out, "Otto! Wait!"

Otto turned to find Twister standing next to Sam and Reggie under an umbrella. "Now what?" he demanded. "Twist, don't let Squid boy and naggy ol' Reggie hold you up! The surf is primed and waiting!"

"Please don't go out there, Otto!" Reggie said, struggling to keep her grip on the umbrella handle as the wind whipped around her body. "You're gonna get really whomped."

Then, as if to back up her words, a huge wave crashed down in front of the group.

"EEEK!" Sam screamed, racing to hide behind Reggie.

"Maybe your sister is right, man," Twister said. "I-I think I'm going to hold off."

Otto's eyes narrowed. "You do what you

want, Twist. Or should I say, *Maurice*."

Twister looked hurt. "Dude! That's most unduly harsh!"

"If the name fits, wear it!" Otto retorted. "Unlike you babies, I'm going surfing with the Rhino! And I'm gonna ride me one of them monster waves!"

"Unless it rides you, first," Reggie said. "Come on, Otto, what are you trying to prove?"

He looked at his sister. "I can do this, Reg. I have to do this!"

Otto then wiped his wet hair back from his forehead, spun on his heel, and jumped into the ocean, paddling as fast as he could after the Rhino.

"Can I have your skateboard?" Twister called.

"Not funny, Twist," Reggie said, already losing sight of her brother in the torrential downpour.

"I can't believe he's actually going to try and surf in this storm," Sam said worriedly. "He could really get hurt."

"You know how stubborn my little brother can be," Reggie said, deciding to take command of the situation. "Okay, reasoning with him didn't work. Time for Plan B."

"You want us to get a net?" Sam asked.

"No, I need you guys to get my dad. I'll stay here and keep an eye on Otto. Once he's busted, he'll come back. But hurry!"

chapter 5

The Rhino was in the zone. The storm was not a problem at all. Ahead of him loomed the monster wave, and all he had to do was focus and ride. To the Rhino it was just another wave going down for the count!

"Hey! Rhino! Wait up!"

The Rhino glanced back to see Otto paddling after him. The surfer's mouth fell open in disbelief. "What are you doing out here, kid? Are you nuts?!" the Rhino yelled, struggling to be heard over the crashing of the water.

"I'm chasing the monster surf, Rhino!" Otto said. "Just like you!"

"Naw, what you're doing is writing a check your tush can't cash, little man," the Rhino called back.

Otto sighed. "Why does everyone always tell me that? I don't even have a checking account. I—uh-oh!"

Without warning a huge wave crashed across the boy's face and body. Otto was now in the middle of the storm. Big Thursday had arrived in full force, and there was no turning back!

🚀 🚀 🚀

Meanwhile, inside the Shore Shack, things were not going well for Ray.

"Looks like you're the old maid, bruddah!" Tito gloated.

Ray tossed the card onto the pile. "Aw, I never was any good at card games, anyway. Give me an outdoor game like volleyball! Then we'll see who the old maid is!"

WHACK! With a wet slap the front door of the Shore Shack flew open. Twister and Sam burst through, accompanied by a barrage of raindrops.

"Ray! Ray! You gotta come quick!" Sam gasped, trying to catch his breath.

Ray was on his feet in an instant. "What? What is it?" he asked.

"It's Otto!" Twister said. "He's . . . he's . . ."

"He's what?" Ray asked as the situation dawned on him. "No, wait. Don't tell me—"

"He's surfin' with the Rhino!" Sam cried.

"Take us there," Ray demanded. He and Tito followed the two boys out toward the beach.

Back in the ocean Otto was seeing more of the wave monster than he ever imagined he would, and all bragging aside, he was starting to worry.

"She's the one!" the Rhino said happily, pointing at the wave as it loomed above them. "Will ya look at that!"

"Oh, man . . . what am I doing out here?" Otto whispered. Deep down, he knew his own taste for thrills drove him to follow in the Rhino's wake.

Otto thought about how his dad had always stressed that a totally rad surfer never ever took unnecessary risks. Now Otto was tired, and cold—and very scared. If only he had listened to his dad!

As the mighty wave continued to rise, Otto and the Rhino split up. Otto paddled to the right, the Rhino to the left.

Otto felt like he was inside a giant washing machine as he was slammed on all sides by the force of the ocean waves.

There was no avoiding the onslaught of water. Otto knew that the only thing he could do was try to stand on his surfboard, keep his feet under him, and maybe he would be able to ride it out.

Otto caught a glimpse of the Rhino out of the corner of his eye—and was shocked to see the Rhino waving at the wave! "Yeah, baby! Come to mama!" Rhino called.

Otto gulped and stopped watching his hero. He had a bigger worry—getting out of this wet mess in a single piece!

He paddled up the face of the wave as quickly as he could, trying to get over the crest of the high-reaching water—but it was too big, too wide, and too fast.

"HELLLLLP!" he screamed. Otto was thrown backward head-over-heels as the huge wave began to break. He was tossed straight over the falls, vanishing after his surfboard into the watery deluge like a piece of scrap paper tossed into the midst of a tornado!

The Rhino popped up on his board, easily riding down the face of the wave. "Yeah, baby! Nobody rides like Rhino!" he bellowed, having the ride of his life.

As for Otto, there was no sign of him in the water.

chapter 6

Back on the beach Ray, Tito, Sam, and Twister raced up in the storm to Reggie. There was a groove in the sand where she had been nervously pacing while waiting for them to arrive.

"Where's Otto?" Ray asked over the howl of the wind. "No, wait. Very dumb question."

Reggie pointed to the giant wave. "He's out there," she replied. "I just lost sight of him. He was across from Rhino."

Everyone in the group stared anxiously out at the ocean.

"I am Rhino! Hear me roar!" the Rhino called, still standing tall on his board, his voice booming out across the thunder of the storm.

"Wow! Look at Rhino go!" an impressed Sam said.

"He is the man on a board," agreed Twister.

"Save the admiration society for later, guys," Reggie said. "We're looking for Otto, remember?"

Just then Tito spotted a familiar shock of red hair break the surface of the dark water behind the Rhino. "Oh, bruddah, look at Otto!" he said, pointing.

"At least he's still keeping his noodle above water," Ray noted. "We'll have to try and paddle out to him. Ready for a swim, Tito?"

"Wet from the rain already, but I could

use a dip, pronto!" Tito answered. Together the two men ran to the edge of the water and dove in, swimming as hard as they could against the approaching waves.

The surf pounded against them as they looked for Otto. The boy's head had been pulled under the water once more. Time was running out!

"Otto!" Ray called loudly. "Answer me, son!"

"Little Rocket bruddah! Where are you?" Tito yelled.

Otto broke the surface of the wave again, his mouth filled with seawater. "Augh! Pitooey! Dad! Tito! HELLLP!" he called.

Ray could hear his son, but couldn't find him in the storm. "Do you see him, Tito?" he shouted. "I've lost sight of him!"

But there was no response.

"Tito?" Ray said, looking all around.

With a chill of fright, he realized that not only could he not see Otto, but Tito seemed to have vanished as well! Ray searched the rainy horizon and the rising and falling waves, his keen eyes darting as he sought any sign of human life.

"Dad!"

Ray turned just in time to see Otto's head pop up in the thrashing water. Without wasting another second, Ray swam over to his son and hugged him tight. Ray could feel Otto's heart pounding against him.

"Th-Thanks for the rescue, Dad," Otto gasped.

"You're welcome, but wait till you get my bill," Ray replied in a calm voice to soothe his frightened son. "Now, grab on to me and everything will be okay. We just—"

KERSPLASSSHHH! Suddenly a huge wave scooped the pair up! It whipped them back and forth toward shore.

"*Glub!* Hold on, son!" Ray cried.

"I'm—*blub*—holdin', Dad!"

Ray and Otto bobbed above the water, and were then sucked back down.

"No! They went under again!" Reggie screamed from the safety of her lookout point on the beach. "I've got to do something!"

"No way," Sam replied, taking her arm and holding fast. "There are enough people out there already."

"Don't worry," Twister said. "If anybody's going to ride these waves back to home base, it's your dad."

They had seen Ray latch on to Otto, but then both Rockets had disappeared again. There was no sign of Tito, either. Only Rhino was still riding high, seeming to enjoy every second of his crazy surfing experience.

Reggie took a deep breath, then held her umbrella firm against the storm. "We'd better back up a bit, guys," she said. "Or we're all going to end up caught in that wave when it comes in!"

The trio retreated to their sand dune just in time. With a watery roar, the monster wave crashed down several feet away, tossing Ray and Otto onto shore.

Reggie, Sam, and Twister ran up to them through the rain.

"Oh, you guys are okay! Oh, man!" Reggie cried as she gave Ray and Otto a big, wet hug.

Twister scanned the water. "Where's Tito?"

Ray looked up as he realized his friend was still lost.

"I don't know where he went, Twist," Ray said. "And it's all my fault."

"I'm sure he's okay, Dad," Otto replied. "He's *gotta* be. . . ."

Then, as if on cue, a familiar voice was

heard above the crashing of the waves and the whistling of the storm winds.

"ALOOOOOHAAAAAAA!"

Everyone gasped, peering out at the ocean at a most amazing sight: There was big Tito—hanging ten on top of Otto's little surfboard!

chapter 7

"I am the Tito!" the Hawaiian hollered, giving the group a thumbs-up as he rode the wave!

"He certainly is!" Ray exclaimed.

"Alohaaa—" Tito started to call again, only this time, the board started to slip away from him and the cry changed into "Aloaaauuhhhugh!"

FOOMP! The water stopped shoreside, and Tito's borrowed board hit the sand! The board dug in and froze in place—but

Tito kept going. He was flying through the air!

"Whoa! Whoa! Whoa!" Tito yelled before plowing right into Ray.

"Ooooof!" Ray said as he fell backward.

"Nice catch, Raymundo," Tito said.

Ray wheezed. "Well, you know what they say, 'Any landing you can walk away from is a good one. . . .' but do you mind getting off me now?"

"Oh, sorry, bro." Tito fell back onto the sand and gazed up at the dark, stormy sky. The rain had let up quite a bit.

Otto sheepishly looked down at Tito, who gave him a half smile. "That was some crazy ride, little Rocket bruddah."

"Sorry, Tito."

"Some crazy ride," Tito said again. "I think I'm going to just lie here for a few hours."

"You bet," Otto said. "Want an umbrella or something?"

"No, thanks. I'm all nice and wet. Why spoil it?"

Ray used Otto's board as a crutch to raise himself up. "That was a nice save on the board, Tito, but I don't think Otto's gong to be needing it for a while. Are you, son?"

Otto stood tall, fully prepared to take his punishment. "No, sir. Someone as reckless as I was today doesn't deserve to surf."

"Accepting responsibility for your actions. I like that," Ray said with a grin. "Good answer."

"I had a good teacher," Otto said, grinning back. "You might have heard of him."

Then, above the crash of the surf, a now familiar bellow erupted. "I . . . am . . . RHINOOOOOOO! Hear me ROARRRRR!"

The scene seemed almost in slow motion as the Rhino came gliding majestically into shore after a perfect ride.

Pausing to pose in front of the group, the Rhino flashed his most handsome smile. "Awesome, wasn't I?"

"That's one way of putting it," Reggie replied.

"Oh, yeah, you the man," Twister said without enthusiasm.

"King Surf," Sam added, not looking at the Rhino.

"You're standing on my stomach," Tito announced.

"Whoops! Sorry, dude," the Rhino said as he stepped off Tito's midsection. "Didn't see you down there."

"'S okay," Tito said. "Just meditating here."

Ray stuck Otto's board into the sand and leaned over. "You know, Otto, I think I'll have a little talk with Rhino about being a role model for kids," he said brightly.

"Um . . . okay," Otto said. He watched nervously as his father walked over to the

Rhino, who was checking out his surfboard.

"Oh, Walter, got a minute?" Ray asked.

"Dude, it's Rhino."

"Whatever. Come here," Ray said as he took the Rhino's arm and walked over behind the sand dune, out of the sight of the kids.

Reggie, Twister, and Sam wondered what the discussion was going to be about.

"I think Dad's mad at Rhino," Otto said.

"You think correctly," Tito said, sitting up.

Moments later, Ray stepped back from around the dune, brushing off his hands.

"What happened to Rhino?" Sam asked.

"Walter, I mean, Rhino, has some thinking to do. We discussed the responsibility of being a role model," Ray answered. "You know, he's really a reasonable, sweet guy once you get to know him."

On the other side of the dune Rhino kicked his feet helplessly as he tried to pull his head out of the sand. Finally with a soft *POP!* he pulled free and shook his head vigorously, trying to shake the sand out of his ears.

"Whoa. Being a role model is hard work," he said.

Otto shoved his hands into his pockets and kicked the ground. "I really messed up, Dad. I should have never been out there. I was in way over my head."

"Now you know your limitations," Ray explained. "Someday you'll be able to ride the big waves. I just hope you learned something today."

Otto thought about his dad's words for a minute. "I know!" he said at last. "Like, I should never bounce checks my tush can't cash!"

"Huh?" Ray replied. "Oh, well, yeah. Almost."

"No, I got it wrong," Otto said, correcting

himself. "I should never bounce my tush on a check, right?"

Ray patted Otto on the head as they walked back toward the Shore Shack. "Sure, son . . . sure."

story #2
POWERGIRL
SURFERS

chapter 1

Otto stepped confidently into the ocean and paddled his board out toward the first breaking wave.

On the beach Reggie, Twister, and Sam watched him get into position, head into the heart of the wave, then rise on his board. Otto rode the crest as easily as he might have walked down a flight of stairs.

"The kid *is* good," Sam admitted.

"Of course he is," said Reggie proudly. "I taught him everything he knows!"

Otto continued his ride, heading down the line and bashing the lip of the wave.

"Rip it! Rip it! Rip it!" Otto chanted softly, focusing on the wave and his board.

Otto's sister and friends cheered him on. Behind them on the shore a hot-pink and purple banner flapped in the ocean breeze. The banner read: OCEAN SHORES SURFIN' SHOOTOUT.

"He makes it look sooo easy," Reggie said.

"Take no prisoners, Otto-man!" Twister called, pumping a fist into the air as Otto took the wave into the shore, staying on top until there was nothing left to catch a ride on. Breathing heavily, he emerged from the surf with board in hand.

"Did you guys see that?" Otto asked excitedly as his friends gathered around.

"You nailed a spot in the finals for sure, dude!" Twister told him, giving Otto a high five. "Lights . . . camera . . . aloooha! The

Otto-matic Machine means business!"

"I agree," a new voice said. "Best surfin' I've seen all day."

The gang turned to face a tall man wearing sunglasses, a white cap, and a Hawaiian shirt. He was carrying a small notebook and a pen.

"I'm Slack Brizack, top reporter for *Gnarly Surf* magazine," he said. "And I think I've just found the subject of my next story!"

chapter 2

Slack Brizack eyed Otto carefully, peering down at the boy from behind his shades. "You're Ray Rocket's son, right?"

"Guilty as charged," Otto said, trying to appear cool but failing miserably in containing his excitement.

Slack extended a hand. "You ever hear of *Gnarly Surf* magazine?" he asked.

Otto shook the reporter's hand and said, "Like, I only eat, drink, and breathe *Gnarly Surf* for breakfast, lunch, and dinner."

Slack nodded. "Three square *Gnarly* meals a day! Excellent!"

"Hey, I can burp-talk 'Gnarly Surf.' Wanna hear?" Twister asked.

"I'll pass," Slack said, dismissing Twister. "Thanks, anyway."

Too late! Twist had already swallowed a double lungful of air and proceeded to croak out a nasty-sounding "Gnar—*brack*—ly Surrrr—*urp*—ffffff!"

Slack winced, then turned back to Otto. "So, Rocket, I'm watching you tear it up out there and I'm thinking maybe I should come back on Sunday with my best photographer and do a *cover story* on a hot young surfer—like you!"

Otto staggered back in disbelief. "Cover? About me? Oh, man!"

"I thought you might dig some publicity," said Slack. "We'll add a double-page spread on your rad life and times in the magazine.

What do you say, kid?" Slack asked.

"Awesome!" Sam said.

"Man, Otto, you would rule the beach!" added Twister.

"Hmm," Reggie muttered, as Otto thought about Slack's offer.

Otto grabbed Reggie's arm. "Can you believe this? Dad is going to trip! A Rocket on the cover of *Gnarly Surf!* I—" And then he suddenly fell silent.

Otto turned back to the reporter. "You know, Slack, all of the Rocket family surfs. What say we let Reg on the cover with me?"

"If he's half as good as you, little dude, no problem," Slack replied breezily. "Who's Reg? Is he your older brother or something?"

"Or something," Reggie said, stepping forward and looking up at the reporter. "Try his older sister."

"Yeah, meet Regina Rocket!" Otto said proudly. "She's a hot surfer too! You should see her shred! She can totally—"

Slack chuckled and patted Reggie on the shoulder. "Her? Shred? Yeah, right . . . now, come on, Otto, stop kidding around. Tell the Slackmeister how long you've been surfing."

Reggie's face reddened. Sam and Twister bit their lower lips a second time and winced again. They knew the signs—Reggie was furious, and when she was upset, everyone knew to stay out of her way!

Reggie poked a finger in Slack's chest and got in the reporter's face. "*We* have been surfing all of *our* lives! Which means *I* have been surfing longer! And for your information, yes, I *do* shred!"

But Slack wasn't intimidated by Reggie's attitude. He simply smiled, showing off two rows of perfect teeth. "Of course you do," he said slowly in a syrupy tone of voice. "But you gotta understand—nobody *really* cares about *girl* surfers—except, maybe, *other* girl surfers."

"*WHAAAT?!*" Reggie shrieked.

"I think I hear my mother calling," Sam whispered, backing up slowly.

"Uh, me too," Twister agreed, tiptoeing away.

Otto stepped in front of his sister and tried to play peacemaker. "Can't you just think about including her, Slack?" he asked. "She's *really* good."

Slack tapped his pen on his notebook and mulled over Otto's request. "Tell you what," he said, "show me a decent surfer who's a girl, and maybe I'll consider it."

"Start considering!" Reggie retorted. "Right here, right now!" She grabbed Otto's board and marched toward the water.

"You gotta admire a gal with spunk," Slack said.

"You do?" Otto asked hopefully.

"Mm-hmm," Slack said. "Too bad I hate spunk."

chapter 3

Slack flipped open his notebook and turned to Otto. "Okay, now that we got rid of her, what's it gonna be, Rocket boy? You ready to be a star?"

Otto peered past Slack at Reggie, who was now paddling toward an approaching wave. "I . . . um . . . I don't know."

Slack closed his notebook and shrugged. "Fine. There are lots of good surfers around Ocean Shores. I'm sure I can find someone else for the cover."

The reporter strolled away, leaving a moody Otto alone to sulk.

Just then Sam and Twister walked up to Otto.

"Good for you, Otto. That guy's a creep," Sam said.

"Who cares? You could be on the cover of *Gnarly Surf*, dude!" Twister replied.

Sam shook his head in disbelief. "Reggie will go ballistic."

"But it's the cover, dude!" Twister argued. "The cover!"

"Family comes first!" Sam said, stomping his foot on the sand.

"Fame comes first!" declared Twister. "Fame and fortune!"

"Feelings," Sam said, "as in your sister's feelings."

"But it's the *cover*! When will you ever get another shot at the cover?" Twister said.

"Shut up, already!" Otto cried, putting

his hands over his ears. "I can't think straight with you two yammering away at me!"

"What's it going to be?" Sam said.

Otto took a deep breath—and sprinted down the beach toward Slack. "Hold up!" Otto called.

Slack paused, and turned around with a knowing smirk. "Change your mind?" he asked. "I figured you would come to your senses."

Otto held out his hand to shake. "Okay. Count me in for the cover."

Slack shook Otto's hand. "Most excellent! Now, let me take a few notes for my story. . . ."

"Yesss!" Twister said, watching the hand-shake from afar. He ran over to congratulate his friend.

Sam stayed where he was, watching as Reggie completed an amazing display of surfing prowess. Unfortunately, he was the only one watching her. Slack had not paid any attention to the exhibition.

Sam walked down to the edge of the water and waited as Reggie came in from her ride. She was well aware that Slack had not bothered to honor Otto's request to watch a skilled girl surfer. "What a jerk!" she said. "That stupid reporter didn't even watch me!"

"Aw, what does he know? You're a girl and you're a great surfer! You're just as good as Otto!" Sam said, trying to cheer Reggie up.

Reggie wasn't buying the kind words. "It makes me so mad! There are so many girls who rip! I know this girl Trish who hangs at Spray Beach, and she rips harder than any guy!"

"Totally," Sam agreed.

"It's a good thing Otto isn't going along

with that jerk!" Reggie ranted. "Who needs *Gnarly Surf* magazine any—hey!"

Reggie had just spotted Otto talking with Slack. "What's Otto doing?" she asked.

"An interview," Sam admitted. "I think he's decided to be the cover boy."

Reggie shoved the nose of Otto's surfboard into the sand and stomped toward her brother.

"See you on Sunday, Slack," Otto agreed, waving good-bye to the reporter. Otto was on cloud nine—for approximately twenty seconds.

"Thanks for nothing!" Reggie yelled at Otto.

"Come on, Reg! Listen—" Otto replied, trying to explain.

Reggie held up her hand. "I don't want to hear it!"

"Well, you're going to anyway," Otto said, digging in his heels. "I told Slack what a great surfer you were, remember?"

"And then you let him dis me! He couldn't even be bothered to watch me surf!"

"But it's the cover, Reg!" Otto pleaded. "It's a once-in-a-lifetime opportunity!"

"Well, get this!" Reggie said. "For the rest of *your* lifetime, do me a major favor and stay out of my face!"

The three boys watched as Reggie stormed off toward the Shore Shack.

"I think that went pretty well, guys," Twister said happily. "Don't you?"

chapter 4

A frowning Reggie stomped into the Shore Shack and took a seat at the counter.

"Wipe out, Reg?" Tito asked as he put an orange sherbet shake down in front of her.

"I wish. Maybe then that dumb writer would have paid attention to what I was doing on the water," she replied.

Ray stepped over and sat down next to Reggie. "Tell us about it," he said.

Reggie gave them the entire scenario, finishing her story with a growl. "It's not fair!"

"I know, hon," Ray agreed. "Otto's gonna have to learn there's more to surfing than some photo spread in *Gnarly Surf* magazine."

Reggie took a final sip and slid the glass across the counter. "Hit me again, Tito," she said, sighing.

"Drowning your sorrows in ice cream isn't the solution," Tito said, taking out a burger patty and placing it on the grill. "You should have a Tito-Titanic Burger-Bomber, okay?"

"Okay, I guess," Reggie muttered, and then started in about her brother again. "That stupid Otto! His head swelled to six times its normal size when that creepy reporter mentioned the cover shot."

Ray leapt to his feet and slapped his hands to the sides of his face. "Did you say 'cover shot?!'" he exclaimed, winking at his daughter. "Wow, now that changes everything!"

"Daa-ad!" Reggie yelled, although she was trying to stifle a giggle.

"Made you laugh," Ray said, sitting down again. "Tito, I'll have what the lady's having. Fix me up with a plate and a shake!"

Tito tossed another patty onto the grill. "You know," he said. "I was once on the cover of *Hawaiian Princess* magazine—but . . . um . . . well, that's another story."

"And we're about to eat," Ray added. "Now, Reg, your brother did stick up for you, didn't he?"

"Yeah," Reggie admitted.

"So, he did try to involve you."

"Doesn't matter," she replied. "I've got to show him and that Slack Brizack that there are tons of great girl surfers."

"Oh, there most certainly are, little one," Tito agreed.

"Did you know any great ones back in the day?" Reggie asked.

Tito nodded. "I did. A long time ago I charged a big, thick, chunky wave with my tandem partner, a woman named Surfin' Sarah Ann!"

"I never heard of her," Reggie said.

"That's because they wouldn't report on girl surfers back then, either," Tito explained. "Ah, you should have seen us. We were known for our style, our grace, and our agility. Me, particularly!"

Ray rubbed the cleft in his chin. "That's funny, Tito. I remember it slightly differently. Didn't you end up falling off the board?"

"Uh . . . did I? I don't recall," Tito replied, turning away to flip the burgers.

"Sure you did . . . and then Surfin' Sarah Ann grabbed you and hoisted you over her head!" Ray said. "Ah, that Sarah. She was a strong, beautiful woman—and a little scary."

"And she always did what she felt she had to do?" Reggie asked.

"That she did," Tito agreed, placing the two burgers down in front of Ray and Reggie.

"Then that's the answer! Thanks, Tito! Thanks, Dad!" Reggie said as she hopped down from the stool and ran out of the restaurant.

"Well, aloha to you, too!" Tito said, shrugging.

"Hey, Reg, don't you want your burger?" Ray called, but she was already gone.

"As the Ancient Hawaiians say, 'Aloha means hello and good-bye, because every farewell is the start of a new day,'" Tito said.

Ray pointed at Reggie's untouched burger. "Now, does this mean more chow for me?"

"Nope," Tito replied, grabbing the burger. "More chow for me!"

chapter 5

Reggie went to get Sam, and together they rode their bikes up the boardwalk to Spray Beach.

"Do you think she's riding today?" Sam asked. "I didn't see her at the Surfin' Shootout tryouts."

"With weather like this? You bet she's around here somewhere!" Reg replied. "And she hates contests. Said she got tired of winning them all the time."

Sam did a double take. "She did?"

Reggie nodded. "Trish was a legend before you moved here from Kansas, Sammy."

"Cool," Sam said. "I can't wait to meet her!"

"Well, here's your chance," Reggie said, pointing to the ocean. "There she is!"

"Whoa!" Sam said. "She rules!"

Tearing up a wave was a girl in a blue swimsuit that matched the color of her surfboard. As Reggie and Sam watched, the girl belly-rode her board to shore after easily nailing a perfect floater.

"Hey, Trish! Got a sec?" Reggie called as she parked her bike next to Sam's.

Trish picked up her board and walked over. "What's up?" she asked.

"We need your help," Reggie said.

"Hi," Sam added, blushing and digging a toe in the sand.

Reggie rolled her eyes. "Sam, this is Trish.

Trish, meet Sam Dullard. We call him 'Squid' for short.

"The Squid! Glad to know you," Trish replied. "So, what's the deal?"

"We're rounding up a bunch of kids to speak out against *Gnarly Surf* 'cause they don't show any girl surfers in their crummy magazine," Reg explained.

"*Gnarly Surf?*" Trish said. "I didn't even know they were still publishing that rag."

"Well, they are! And we've got to show them that us girls mean business! Can I count on you?"

Trish grinned. "Hey, Reggie, I'd love to, but I just like riding waves, not making them, you know?"

"But—"

"Later, girlfriend," Trish said as she headed back to the ocean.

"She's beautiful," Sam sighed.

"And she's the best surfer in town!"

Reggie said as they walked back over to the bike rack. "If Trish doesn't come out for the protest, nobody will!"

Sam sat down on a bench and pondered the situation. "We're gonna need some major assistance if we're gonna pull this off."

"Someone who will support the cause!" Reggie agreed.

"Someone who can organize—and, even better, someone with food!" Sam added.

Suddenly they heard the loud *HONK! HONK!* of a car horn. Reggie and Sam turned to find Violet Stimpleton, the Rockets' next-door neighbor.

"Hello there, children!" Violet called. "Do you need a lift back to Ocean Shores?"

Sam and Reggie both blinked.

"I think our prayers have been answered," Reggie said. And sure enough, after listening to Reggie's story, Violet was more than happy to help her young neighbor.

The next day Violet drove back to Spray Beach with Sam and Reggie in the front seat of her car. In the back seat and trunk were homemade snacks from Violet's kitchen!

Reggie had spent the night calling every girl surfer she knew and inviting them to a meeting. Whether anyone would show up remained to be seen. Reggie chose Spray Beach over her usual stomping grounds at Ocean Shores to avoid prying eyes and because she hoped Trish still might join her cause.

"Oh, I haven't been out on the beach since I was a young girl," Violet said as she drove along the Pacific Coast Highway. "But I do like to look at the pretty sunsets. My Merv has a thing about sand. He doesn't like the taste."

"Me either," Sam admitted with a shudder.

Since Sam was prone to wipeouts on a regular basis, he always had some grit trapped between his teeth.

"I think it's incredible that you're fighting for something you believe in," Violet said to Reggie. "The important thing is not to just accept things the way they are."

Reggie smiled. "You know what? You're pretty smart, Mrs. Stimpleton."

Violet winked. "Of course I am. Left that poopy ol' Merv at home, didn't I?"

The older woman pulled her car to a stop at the meeting place Reggie had selected. Across the way there was a vista of clear water, sun, and fantastic ocean waves.

And riding the waves was a pack of girl surfers!

"They came, they came!" Sam burbled happily.

"Look at all of them!" Reggie said in a

stunned voice. "It's incredible!"

Violet got out of the car and gave a wild cry. "Cowabunga! Surf's up, dudettes!"

"Mrs. Stimpleton . . . do you surf?" Sam asked in amazement.

"No, dear, but it's never too late to try," Violet giggled. "Now, you two run along and mingle while I set up the table."

One by one, the girl surfers came in and were introduced to Reggie's plan to boycott *Gnarly Surf*. As Reggie talked with the girls, Violet put her catering skills to work. She soon had an interesting-looking and colorfully named spread on a picnic table.

There were tall, frosty glasses of "Peanut-Butter-Pineapple Smoothies" with curly straws, "Clam Sand-Wishes" with freshly dug clams, and for dessert, "Jellyfish Jelly Rolls" filled with grape-flavored "tentacles!"

Reggie ran up to Violet. "Are you ready?" she asked.

"Cowabunga! Oh, I just love saying that," Violet said, laughing. "I'm ready to go, dear. How is the recruiting going?"

Reggie shrugged. "They seem interested. I just wish Trish was here."

Violet patted Reggie on the arm. "Chin up, hon. The day isn't over yet!"

chapter 6

Once word spread that the free food was ready, the girls descended on Violet's picnic like a swarm of hungry ants! As Reggie watched the girls dig in she couldn't help but think that girl surfers not only played as hard as boy surfers, but they also had equally large appetites!

Violet saw Sam standing off to one side. "What's the matter?" she asked.

"Well, since I'm a guy, I figured I'd have to wait until all these girls eat, right?"

Violet laughed. "No, Sam. We're all people here. You may dig in too!"

Sam didn't hesitate. "Thank you!" he said, then grabbed a plate and loaded up. Stuffing three Jellyfish Jelly Rolls into his mouth, Sam chewed happily as three surfers came over to him.

"Uh . . . hi!" Sam said between mouthfuls. "Welcome to the girl power-surf-lunching . . . thing."

The girls giggled. Then one of them said, "I'm Sherry. What's your name?"

"I'm Squid," Sam said. "I mean, Sam. They . . . uh . . . call me Squid."

"Glad to meet you, Squid," she said.

Sam gulped, then blushed.

Just then Reggie climbed up on the now-empty picnic table. "May I have your attention please! Thank you all for coming today. There are a lot of guy surfers out there who think they're something special. So, basically, what we can accomplish together as a force is to show the world what power-girl surfers can do!"

Sherry raised her hand. "Is Trish coming?" she asked.

"I'd like to think so," Reggie replied, "but don't get your hopes up."

A murmur went through the crowd.

"You're losing 'em," Sam whispered.

Reggie waved her arms and the group fell silent. "Look, it's about showing everyone that girls surf hard too, okay? We deserve to be recognized! We're calling it, 'A Peaceful Surfing Expression Session Protest of the Male-Dominated Surf-Magazine Industry.' What do you think?"

The gathered group of girls blinked as Reggie waited for a response.

"Well, first I think you need a catchier title," Trish said as she appeared from the back of the crowd and walked up to Reggie.

"Does this mean you're in?" Reggie asked. Trish nodded. "Let's rip!"

"Cowabunga!" Violet cried. "Back to Ocean Shores, gals! I'm driving!"

And less than an hour later at Ocean Shores, Ray Rocket pushed back his white sailor's cap and took in the mob scene on the beach. Moments before, it had been standing room only inside the Shore Shack! He had left the restaurant for some air, but even out here on the sand, one had to fight for a spot to spread a beach blanket.

Tito soon joined him. He had to close the Shack because they had run out of food! The pantries were bare and the soda fountains were empty. They were even picked clean of the little ketchup and mustard packets.

"Reggie sure got a lot of people to stand up and take notice," Ray mused. "I've never seen so many girl surfers on the water in my life!"

"Like the Ancient Hawaiians say, 'Never

provoke the wrath of a ten-year-old *wahine*. You always get more than you bargained for,'" Tito said.

Ray nodded toward a tall figure in dark sunglasses carrying a notebook. "That must be the reporter for *Gnarly Surf* magazine," he said. "Here comes the moment of truth."

Slack gawked at the scene on the beach in total befuddlement. Behind him, Odell, his ace photographer, was also amazed.

"Look at this. It's incredible!" Slack said. "Odell, start taking pictures! I'm going to find that Rocket girl!"

Odell waded into the crowd and began shooting photos of the girls on the waves.

Spotting Sherry and her friends with their surfboards, Slack stopped to talk to them. "Can I ask you lovely ladies a few questions?"

Sherry pointed to her left. "Check with The Squid."

"The what?" Slack asked.

"The Squid," Sam replied, turning to face Slack. Sam was wearing a snazzy jacket and sunglasses similar to Slack's attire. "Now, how can I help you, sir?"

"You can help by moving out of the way, junior," Slack sneered, taking out his press card and shoving it into Sam's face. "I'm Slack Brizack, with *Gnarly Surf* magazine. Maybe you've heard of me?"

"Can't say as I have, Slap—"

"That's Slack."

"Whatever. Sorry, but no can do. This event is being exclusively covered by another magazine," Sam said. "A magazine edited *and* published by a powergirl surfer named Reggie Rocket. Maybe you've heard of her?"

chapter 7

Sam peered at Slack. "This is an exclusive for Reggie Rocket's 'zine."

"WHAAT?!" Slack screeched.

Across the beach, Otto's ears perked up. "That sounded like Slack!" he said to Twister.

The two friends were carrying Otto's board and looking for the reporter and his photographer. Otto was getting panicky. He had been watching all the girl surfers gathering on the beach, enjoying the hot sun and the cool surf, and knew that his sister had something to do with it.

Twister spotted Slack and Odell and waved. "Yo, Otto! Slack and his picture-taking guy are over there!"

"Good, good. Man, look at those girls rip!" Otto said nervously, staring out at the girls riding the waves. "I hope this doesn't blow my cover story with the magazine!"

"Chill, dude. The cover's not dead," Twister said easily. "Just go out there and show them what a real champ surfer is like!"

"A real chump is more like it," Reggie said, walking up behind Otto and Twister. Trish and Sherry were with her, and all three girls looked very confident.

Otto, however, felt very uncomfortable. "Look, Reg, just stay out of this," he said.

"Yeah!" Twister said. "I can't believe you're so jealous you're trying to ace Otto out of the cover spot!"

Reggie held up her hands in a truce motion. "Look, I'm not here to mess up Otto's cover or any of that. Trish and Sherry here just wanna challenge you two to a peaceful, non-competitive, head-to-head display of surfing talent. Deal?"

"No problemo," Twister replied, accepting the challenge. "You guys, er, I mean, girls, are about to learn a lesson."

"See you on the water, boys," Sherry said with a giggle as the girls walked away.

"I'll take Sherry, you can handle Trish," Twister said.

"Sure," Otto answered with a nervous quiver in his voice. "But I hate that I gotta surf against Trish. She's really good."

"So are you, man!" Twister said. "So are you!"

Moments later, the challenge was in full swing. Twister and Sherry were coming in on the same wave, which meant they were both in the running. But Twister was bringing up the rear and eating the spray kicked out from behind Sherry's board!

"I can't see . . . ," Twister muttered, trying to keep his footing as he chose his path on the wave.

Everyone on the beach could see that the clear winner was Sherry. And there was no debating it an instant later when Twister wiped out. Sherry couldn't resist surfing rings around his bobbing head. The crowd laughed and cheered as she rode the wave onto the beach.

The second pair of surfers came up behind, riding on their own wave. Trish and Otto were side by side, each of them evenly matched as they ripped their paths across the water.

If Trish zigged, Otto zagged. If she dipped, he dodged. The duo put on an amazing show of surfing. Despite any differences of opinion, their movements on the water seemed to complement each other, as though they were meant to surf as one beautifully choreographed unit.

Then, without warning, Otto's wave broke beneath his board, and he plummeted into the water. Seeing her opponent vanish, Trish twisted and pulled into the barrel of the wave, skidding along like a brightly colored stone across the surface of the ocean.

The contest was over. As Trish and Otto both swam their way back to the beach, everyone knew the powergirl surfers had outsurfed the boys.

Reggie ran out to give Trish a hug, with Slack and Odell close on her heels. Reggie gave the reporter her best glare. "Girls can't surf, huh?"

"Whatever gave you that idea?" Slack replied smoothly. "I always knew girl surfers could shred. Hey, how about your own column in our magazine?"

Reggie and Trish walked away from him. "Sorry, Slack, but my 'zine comes first. You can read all about it if you want to subscribe."

"Um . . . Mr. Brizack?" Otto said. "Do you still want to take my pic—"

"No, thanks," Slack replied. "Sorry, kid, but boy surfers are old news. I've got a certain girl I want to have photographed."

"Dream on," Trish said. "I'm already booked."

Slack threw up his hands in frustration. "Can somebody tell me what this was all about?" he asked his photographer.

"Beats me, man. All I do is take pictures," Odell replied as the pair walked toward the pier.

Otto caught up with Reggie and tapped her on the shoulder. "I . . . um . . . just wanted to say I'm sorry."

Reggie punched Otto on the shoulder. "For what? You didn't do anything wrong, little brother. It was that idiot from *Gnarly Surf* that caused all the problems."

"You think?" Otto said, feeling a little better.

"Sure! Hey, forget about his dumb mag! There's always room for you on the cover of my 'zine!" she said.

"You mean it?"

"Come on, everybody," Sam called, holding up his camera. "Let's get a group shot for Reggie's 'zine!"

Everyone gathered for the picture, including all the girl surfers, Ray, Tito, Otto, and Twister. Sam stuck the camera on a tripod and hit the timer, then ran to stand in the front row with his friends.

"Okay, on three, say cheese," Sam told the group. "One, two . . ."

Reggie lunged out and grabbed Violet,

pulling her into the photo at the very last second.

"Three!" Sam yelled.

"Cheese!" everyone shouted, except Violet, who cried, "Cowabunga!"

Everybody laughed. The cover shot for Reggie's 'zine was perfect!